**Teggs is no ordinary dinosaur—
he's an astrosaur!**

Captain of the amazing spaceship DSS *Sauropod*, he goes on dangerous missions, fighting evil with the help of his faithful crew, Gipsy, Arx, and Iggy!

ASTROSAURS
BOOK TWO

The Hatching Horror

BY STEVE COLE

ILLUSTRATED BY CHARLIE FOWKES

Aladdin Paperbacks
New York • London • Toronto • Sydney

For Cassie and Nathan

ALADDIN PAPERBACKS
An imprint of Simon & Schuster Children's Publishing Division
1230 Avenue of the Americas, New York, NY 10020
Text copyright © 2005 by Steve Cole
Illustrations copyright © 2005 by Charlie Fowkes
Originally published in Great Britain in 2005 by Red Fox, an imprint of Random House Children's Books
Published by arrangement with Rocket Editorial Ltd.
First U.S. edition 2006
All rights reserved, including the right of reproduction in whole or in part in any form.
ALADDIN PAPERBACKS and colophon are trademarks of Simon & Schuster, Inc.
Designed by Steve Kennedy
The text of this book was set in ITC Legacy Serif Book.
Manufactured in the United States of America
First Aladdin Paperbacks edition June 2006
10 9 8 7 6 5 4 3 2
Library of Congress Control Number 2005930114
ISBN-13: 978-0-689-87842-8
ISBN-10: 0-689-87842-7

WARNING!

THINK YOU KNOW ABOUT DINOSAURS?

THINK AGAIN!

The dinosaurs . . .

Big, stupid lumbering reptiles. Right?

All they did was eat, sleep, and roar a bit. Right?

Died out millions of years ago when a big meteor struck Earth. Right?

Wrong!

The dinosaurs weren't stupid. They may have had small brains, but they used them well. They had big thoughts and big dreams.

By the time the meteor hit, the last dinosaurs had already left Earth forever. Some breeds had discovered how to travel through space as early as the Triassic period, and were already enjoying a new life among the stars.

No one has found evidence of dinosaur technology yet. But the first fossil bones were found only in 1787, and new finds are being made all the time. The proof is out there, buried in the ground.

And the dinosaurs live on, way out in space, even now. They've settled down in a place they call the Jurassic Quadrant, and over the last sixty-five million years they've continued to evolve. . . .

The dinosaurs we'll be meeting are part of a special group called the Dinosaur Space

Service. Their job is to explore space, to go on exciting missions, and to fight evil and protect the innocent!

These heroic herbivores are not just dinosaurs.

They are *astrosaurs*!

NOTE: The following story has been translated from secret Dinosaur Space Service records. Earthling dinosaur names are used throughout, although some changes have been made for easy reading.

THE CREW OF THE DSS SAUROPOD

Teggs Stegosaur,
Captain

Arx Orano,
First Officer

Gipsy Saurine,
Communications
Officer

Iggy Tooth,
Chief Engineer

Jurassic Quadrant

Ankylos

Steggos

Diplox

INDEPENDENT
DINOSAUR
ALLIANCE

vegetarian
sector

Squawk
Major

DSS
UNION OF
PLANETS

PETROSAUR

Corytho

Lambeos

Tri System

Iguanos

Aqua Minor

SEA

OUTER SPACE

Geldos Cluster

Teerex Major

ympus

Planet Sixty

TYRANNOSAUR TERRITORIES

carnivore sector

Raptos

THEROPOD EMPIRE

Megalos

vegmeat zone
(neutral space)

E SPACE

Pliosaur Nurseries

Not to scale

Chapter One

THE EDGE OF EGG-STINCTION!

In a very big hall full of very big dinosaurs, a very big announcement was about to be made.

The Hall of Learning on the planet Odo Minor had never been more packed. Doctors, professors, scientists, TV cameras—they were all squashed up together. The sound of excited dinosaur chatter filled the hall. What was the big news? What had the great Professor Sog discovered now? Two people in the hall already knew. And one of them didn't seem to care very much.

"I don't see why we had to come all this way!" grumbled Captain Teggs Stegosaur. "I haven't been in a learning hall since I passed my astrosaur exams!"

"Be patient, Captain," his

companion, Gipsy, whispered. "As soon as the talk's over, our mission can begin!"

"About time too," Teggs declared. He was a captain in the Dinosaur Space Service, and he lived for adventure. With his brave crew of astrosaurs he traveled through space in the DSS *Sauropod*, the finest ship in the Jurassic Quadrant.

Gipsy, a stripy hadrosaug, was his communications officer. She and Teggs had come here to escort Professor Sog back to the *Sauropod*—along with some very special guests. . . .

She knew her crewmates would be busy up in orbit. Arx Orano, Teggs's brainy triceratops first officer, would be checking over the *Sauropod*'s systems. And Iggy Tooth, the tough iguanodon engineer, would be stoking the ship's mighty engines.

Their latest voyage into outer space would be their longest yet.

"At last," cheered Teggs, making Gipsy jump. "Here comes Professor Sog now!"

Sog was a small twittery old creature who belonged to a species called compsognathus. The audience hooted and stamped their feet politely as the funny little figure walked onto the stage. He stopped beside a mysterious lumpy bundle hidden beneath a black blanket.

A great hush fell over the hall. The dinosaurs waited breathlessly for the professor's words.

Sog struggled to put on a small pair of spectacles. He had trouble reaching his head since his arms were so short. But finally he managed it, and he peered round at the curious crowd.

"Welcome, my friends," he cried. "You are about to hear of a most exciting discovery!"

A bright light started glowing above his head. Seconds later a hologram of a large long-necked dinosaur appeared. It looked a bit like a stegosaurus but with a longer neck and tail, and no spiky plates running down its back.

"This is a plateosaurus," said Sog. "Sweet, peaceful—and almost totally extinct."

"Extinct?" asked a puzzled journalist in the crowd.

Sog nodded sadly. "Their species has almost completely died out."

"Dined out?" asked Teggs, perking up. He was famous for his large appetite—some said it was the largest in the whole Dinosaur Space Service. "Dined out where? Can we come too?"

"Not dined out, *died* out!" groaned Gipsy.

Professor Sog continued his talk. "As you all know, we dinosaurs left Earth long ago. We escaped in spaceships before the meteor struck, never to return. In those days there were many plateosaurus. Nowadays there are hardly any left."

"Why?" someone called.

"Homesickness," said Sog simply. "At first they settled on a fine planet called Platus. But they didn't like it as much as Earth, so they tried to return." He shook his head sadly. "Their space fleet flew into a cosmic storm. Many of their ships were destroyed. The few survivors limped back to Platus . . . to find that *T. rex*es had taken over."

The audience murmured their disapproval.

"I remember reading about that," whispered Teggs. "The *T. rex*es wouldn't budge. There was a big battle."

Gipsy nodded sadly. "And the plateosaurus lost."

"Other vegetarian races came to their aid," the professor went on. "As you know, they joined together and formed the Dinosaur Space Service, to protect all plant-eaters. In the end they kicked the *T. rex*es off Platus. But the little planet had been almost ruined by war."

The hologram switched off above Sog's head. "The plateosaurus species never recovered from the tragedy. Today only a tiny handful survive." He shuffled closer to the black bundle beside him. "But now I bring new hope!"

He clamped his jaws down on the blanket and whipped it away. Beneath it was a pile of nine large white eggs. The audience burst out in gasps and hoots. Flying reptiles flapped nearer with their TV cameras to get a closer look. "Plateosaurus eggs!" cried the little professor. "Discovered in a wrecked space-ship far out in the Jurassic Quadrant. That ship was a victim of the cosmic storm. It has drifted through space for thousands of years. But the eggs survived—completely frozen!"

The great hall filled with excited mutterings.

Professor Sog held up his feeble arms for quiet. "As you know, when it comes to hatching, I am something of an expert. . . ."

"*Eggs*-pert, more like!" Teggs chuckled.

"I was asked to study these old, old eggs," said Sog proudly. "And now that the eggs have thawed out, I believe they will soon hatch! The plateosaurus race *will* live on!"

The audience cheered and stamped their feet so hard that the floor shook.

"That's where we come in!" cried Teggs, rising to his feet. He flexed his long, bony tail, and knocked two elderly triceratops off their stools. "Oops!"

Sog frowned at the commotion. "Is that Captain Teggs?"

"Speaking!" he called cheerily as Gipsy helped up the doddery dinosaurs. "Hello, everyone. It's my mission to take the professor, the eggs, and two plateosaurus guardians to a far-off world called Platus Two, a place where their race can make a fresh start!"

Ka-Boom!

Suddenly the enormous wooden doors at the front of the hall were kicked open. The great hall rang with gasps of shock from the startled crowd.

"Is that a fact?"

Teggs narrowed his eyes. In the doorway

stood a dozen small, ugly creatures. Their small turtlelike heads bobbed about on scrawny necks.

One of the creatures darted toward the stage. "A fresh start for these lovely little hatchlings?" he sneered. He shoved Professor Sog aside. "I don't think so! Not now the oviraptors are here!"

"Oviraptors?" Teggs frowned.

"Uh-oh!" Gipsy turned to Teggs in alarm. "They're nest-raiders! Egg-stealers!"

"We've got to stop them!" yelled Teggs. But he was blocked in on all sides by shocked old dinosaurs.

"I am Prince Goopo, and these are my royal brothers!" The oviraptor snatched up a plateosaurus egg and caressed it with his long, bony fingers. "Eggs are our favorite food, and eggs as rare as *these* will make a meal fit for a king—*and* his princes!" He threw back his head and laughed. "Forget your mission, Captain Teggs. The only place these eggs are going is *into our bellies*!"

Chapter Two

THE EGG-SNATCHERS

"Grub's up, lads!" yelled Prince Goopo.

The oviraptors raced into the learning hall. They moved like lightning. In a second they had stolen every last egg. Then they charged back out through the double doors.

"No!" yelled Teggs. "Get out of my way! They mustn't take the eggs!" He started pushing his way through the dinosaur audience. "You, near the front—stop them!"

But no one paid any notice. They were rooted to the ground with shock at what they had just seen.

"Captain, wait!" called Gipsy.

"Catch up with me, Gipsy!" Teggs had made it through the crowd, and now he was tearing down the aisle after the egg-snatchers.

With a crash he burst out of the learning hall and into the beautiful snowy gardens. He shivered. Winter on Odo Minor was long and cold, and Teggs wished he'd worn his battle armor over his uniform, to keep out the chill.

The learning hall was built on a high hilltop with a terrific view. But one glance at the churned-up snow at his feet told Teggs where the speedy oviraptors had gone—straight down the hillside.

He charged off after them. Then a small oviraptor popped out from behind a tree—with a laser gun!

Zzzapp! A white-hot laser beam shot over Teggs's head.

"Thanks for warming me up!" he called as he dived for the cover of a nearby bush.

"Just stay where you are, please!" said the oviraptor. He didn't sound as fierce as his brother had on the stage. "I hate guns, and I'm a lousy shot."

Teggs frowned. "So why don't you just put down the gun and let me come out?"

"I'd love to," sighed the oviraptor. "But I can't. Goopo would throw a fit. He told me to stop anyone from following us while he fetches the ship."

Teggs chewed some frozen leaves for extra strength. "Do you always do what your brother tells you?" he asked, creeping quietly closer.

"Goopo's the eldest. He'll be king someday." The little figure sighed. "I'm Prince Shelly, the youngest—so I never get any say in what goes on. Now, stay back! I don't want to hurt you!"

"That makes two of us!" called Teggs. Slowly

his big, bony tail snaked out from the under-growth and curled itself around Prince Shelly. . . .

"Got you!" Teggs cried.

The oviraptor gasped as Teggs's tail tight-ened round him—he was trapped!

Teggs dragged his prisoner over to the top of the steep hillside. Goopo and his brothers were nearing the bottom of the slope. Soon they would vanish into the woods, and Teggs would lose them.

He dangled Shelly over the edge of the hill-side. "You know, I think it's time you caught up with your brothers." He grinned. "There's *snow* time to lose!"

With that, Teggs flung Shelly down the hill-side after his brothers. The raptor hit the snow with a yelp. Unable to stop himself, he rolled over and over. And as he rolled, he gathered snow—faster and faster. Soon he looked like a giant squawking snowball. As he tumbled

toward the fleeing oviraptors, he got bigger and rounder and heavier . . .

Until finally—*splat*! The snowball rolled right over Goopo and his brothers, squashing them into the snow.

"Direct hit!" cheered Teggs. Then he sledded down the hill on his tummy to round up the oviraptors and recover the eggs. Luckily, the soft snow had stopped them from breaking—and the oviraptors were unharmed too.

Up close they were not pretty creatures. Their jaws were wide and toothless—instead of teeth, two bony prongs stuck out from the roof of their mouths to crack open their food. Each of the creatures had a high, narrow crest rising up from his head.

Teggs smiled at the dazed reptiles. "That should cool you off till the space police arrive!"

"Curse you, Captain!" snarled Prince Goopo, half-buried by snow. "I command you to release us in the name of our king!"

"No way," said Teggs. "Anyway, I'm sure your king would be very cross if he knew you were stealing such important eggs!"

"Pah!" cried Goopo. "It was his idea! King Albu will kill us if we don't bring him those eggs!"

"He'll fry us with butter!" twittered an oviraptor.

"He'll boil us in salty water for three minutes!" moaned another.

"And then he'll crack our heads with a big spoon!" quaked one more.

"It's quite exhausting," sighed Prince Shelly, still stuck in his giant snowball. "My brothers and I are sent out round the universe in search of tasty new treats for the royal menu. Goopo's right. If we fail . . . the king will have us served with toast!"

Just then, Gipsy came scampering down the hill. "There you are, Captain!" She beamed when she reached the bottom. "I see you've caught the thieves!"

Teggs winked at her. "Better still, the eggs are safe and sound!"

Gipsy frowned. "But, Captain—"

Whatever Gipsy said, Teggs didn't hear it. For with a mighty roar of engines, a strange spaceship rose up into the sky above the forest. It was a long, narrow rocket with two spinning engines at one end, like an enormous eggbeater.

Goopo laughed. "Using Shelly to squash us was a good trick, Captain," he said. "But Prince Hibbit was too quick for you! He got away to the woods and fetched the ship!"

Teggs and Gipsy backed away as the spaceship came in to land. Prince Hibbit was leaning out of the window, making rude faces. The heat from the ship's whisking engines soon melted the nearby snow, and his brothers shook themselves free.

Hibbit fired a laser bolt at Teggs. It missed by less than one inch. He and Gipsy were forced back.

"Get on board, brothers!" Goopo cried. "We

won't be cracked, scram-
bled, and mixed
with mayon-
naise *this* day!"

In the wink of
an eye the soggy
oviraptors had
bundled back on
board with the stolen
eggs. Shelly was the last
inside. With a sad little wave
at Teggs and Gipsy, he vanished into the ship.
It took off at once.

Teggs spoke into the communicator
strapped to his leg. "Teggs to *Sauropod*! Arx,
can you hear me? An oviraptor ship is getting
away! Stop them!" He looked helplessly at
Gipsy. "I don't believe it! I've let them take the
eggs—I've failed!"

Chapter Three

EXPECT THE UN-*EGGS*-PECTED!

On the flight deck of the DSS *Sauropod*, high above the planet, Arx Orano heard his captain's cry.

"Quick!" the triceratops barked at his flight crew. "Switch on the scanners! Find that spaceship!"

The flight crew were dimorphodon, highly trained flying reptiles. They

clucked and flapped about the grassy walls of
the dinosaur spaceship, pulling levers and
flicking switches.

The scanner soon showed the oviraptor ship
soaring away at top speed.

"Fire lasers!" Arx ordered.

Beams of light fired from the *Sauropod*. But
the oviraptor ship quickly whisked away out
of range. Not a single shot found its mark.

Arx sighed and nudged the communicator
with his nose horn. "Captain? This is Arx. I'm
afraid the oviraptors were too quick for us.
They've got away!"

. . .

Captain Teggs felt awful as he walked back to the Hall of Learning. His head hung down in shame.

Gipsy patted him on the side of his neck with a gentle claw. "It's all right, Captain," she said. "There's nothing to worry about!"

"Oh, yeah?" Teggs waved his spiky tail toward the crowds that were starting to spill out from the hall. "Let's see if *they* agree with you!"

Professor Sog was leading his fellow dinosaurs outside. The perky little reptile was hopping about with excitement.

"Well done, Captain!" he chirped. "Your concern was very convincing. Those oviraptors are bound to think they've stolen the *real* eggs!"

Teggs stared at him, wide-eyed. "What do you mean?"

"Those eggs on the stage weren't the real eggs!" Sog chuckled. "They were just props! I brought them along to spice up my talk."

Teggs whooped with relief. "Then where *are* the real eggs?"

"Here!" came a low, lazy voice from the crowd. Two large long-necked creatures stomped into view. Teggs recognized them from the professor's hologram—they were plateosaurus. Each carried a large shiny box around its neck.

"I am Coo," said one of the dinosaurs.

"And I am Dippa," said the other, a female. "We are the guardians of the eggs."

Coo bobbed his head at the box round Dippa's neck. "I watch her eggs."

"And I watch his," Dippa explained.

"So now the mission can begin!" Professor Sog was still merrily leaping about. "Oh, I'd love to see King Albu's face when he tries to eat those eggs!"

. . .

Way out in space, at the sticky center of his royal ship, King Albu sat waiting on his golden throne. Thick drool bubbled out of his mouth and stained his royal robes at the thought of his next meal—fried plateosaurus eggs on toast!

King Albu waited.

And waited.

His tummy rumbled loud enough to make the walls shake. And *still* he waited.

At last King Albu could bear it no more. He turned to the nearest slave and shouted: "Fetch me Prince Goopo—now!"

The slave rushed from the room. Less than a minute later Prince Goopo crawled into the room. He looked very worried.

"Where are my eggs?" hissed King Albu.

Prince Goopo gulped. "I think . . . er . . . I think Cook was having a little trouble bringing out their full flavor. . . ."

"Fetch me the cook at once!" screamed King Albu.

Prince Goopo crawled out of the room at top speed. In seconds he had returned with the cook, who looked red-faced and nervous.

"Where's my supper?" roared the king.

"Erm . . ." The cook crossed his legs like he needed to go to the toilet. "They are . . . er . . . very tough to cook."

"So?" growled King Albu.

"Just serve 'em up as they are!"

"Forgive me, Your Egginess," said the cook. "But I really don't think—"

"Look, Cook. I like 'em soft. I like 'em hard. I like sucking out the yolk with a straw. I like paddling in the egg whites then licking my feet clean."

The slaves nodded solemnly. They had seen him do such things lots of times.

"I like 'em raw. I like 'em fried. I like 'em thin. I like 'em wide." King Albu narrowed his eyes and widened his mouth. "In short, *I like my eggs*, Cook! And I want a piled-up plate of plateosaurus eggs right now!"

The cook sighed and went outside.

He returned with a silver trolley piled high with a grassy salad—and several giant eggs.

"At last!" the king said, drooling. He grasped an egg in both hands. Then he opened his mouth as wide as it would go, and popped it inside.

Where it stuck!

The egg could not be crushed or chewed or

32

slurped down or guzzled. It stuck right in his throat. King Albu's scaly neck looked like a snake that had swallowed a soccer ball!

"Urph!" he choked. "That's not an egg! It's a *rock*! A painted rock!" He ran around, clutching the large lump in his neck. "You idiot, Goopo! I send you out for eggs and you bring back *boulders*!"

With a strangled yell, King Albu coughed up the enormous fake egg and kicked it across the room.

"My stomach wants plateosaurus eggs!" he panted. "And my stomach will not take no for an answer! Get your brothers together, Goopo. We're going to get our hands on those eggs—whatever it takes!"

Chapter Four

THE LONG, LONG JOURNEY

Back on Odo Minor, Iggy the engineer was waiting for his captain in the *Sauropod*'s shuttle. When Teggs poked his head through the door, the iguanodon saluted stiffly.

"Ready for boarding, Captain!" he cried.

"It's going to be a tight squeeze, Iggy!" said Teggs, and he grinned. He came aboard, with Gipsy close behind.

Then Coo and Dippa squeezed in through the shuttle's doorway. They shuffled close together, and Professor Sog hopped aboard beside them.

"I still can't believe the oviraptors went to all that trouble just to steal a lot of painted rocks!" Teggs said, laughing. "That'll give King Albu an upset tummy!"

"It sure will." Gipsy laughed as the shuttle blasted off into space. "And meanwhile we'll make sure the *real* eggs reach Platus Two—safe and sound and ready for hatching!"

Soon the *Sauropod* was racing through space.

On the flight deck Teggs sat in the control pit. A feeling of excitement was building in his belly. His mission had begun. And with the eggs almost ready to hatch, there was no time to lose!

Arx turned on the scanner. A tiny star gleamed in the darkness of space. "That's where we're headed," he said. "The very edge of the galaxy."

Professor Sog nodded his little head. "I'm looking forward to seeing Platus Two!"

Gipsy wrinkled her snout, puzzled. "You mean you haven't been there before?"

"No one's been there for hundreds of years," Sog told her. "Not since it was first discovered by the Jurassic Explorers."

"Wow," breathed Teggs. The Jurassic Explorers were his heroes. They were the reason he had become an astrosaur. Long before he was born, they had discovered and mapped the entire Jurassic Quadrant, where all dinosaurs now lived. The only thing they had never found was a star dragon—a huge winged animal that was said to live somewhere in space. It was Teggs's dream that maybe one day he would find a star dragon himself.

"Why has no one ever gone to live on Platus Two?" asked Gipsy.

"It's too small and far away from everywhere else," said Sog.

"So we'll be the first space-ship to go there in centuries!" Teggs realized.

Arx nodded. "I wonder what it's like there."

"It'll be lovely, just you wait and

see!" Sog smiled. "The explorers planted lots of seeds there. After hundreds of years it should be very green indeed!" He chuckled. "Yes, Platus Two may be too far away to matter to most dinosaurs. But it's the perfect spot for a small herd of peaceful plateosaurus!"

"Hope so," sighed Coo. "A new home would be nice, wouldn't it Dippa?"

"It would, Coo," Dippa agreed.

Just then the ship shook with a sudden *clunk*! The dimorphodon flight crew squawked and then flapped in panic around the room.

"Battle stations!" cried Teggs.

Arx squinted at his instruments. "No sign of hostile ships," he reported. "Only a meteor bouncing off the side of the ship."

"Oh," said Teggs, a tiny bit disappointed.

"Funny," said Arx. "It seems to be following us."

"It must have got caught in our gravity field," said Professor Sog.

"I suppose so," Arx replied. "But I've never known a meteor do that before."

"We're out in deep space now," said Gipsy. She looked a bit spooked. "Who knows what we'll find out here?"

"We'll find Platus Two, that's what!" said Sog firmly. "Don't let your imagination run away with you, child!"

But as the *Sauropod* sped on to its destination, Gipsy found it was hard not to.

Days passed, and the stars grew fewer and fainter.

Space grew blacker and blacker.

And Captain Teggs began to grow bored. For the first few days he'd kept a careful watch for star drag- ons. But he could find no sign of one any- where.

By the end of the first week the scanner was showing nothing but black- ness. The *Sauropod* was like a big fish swimming through the darkest sea in the uni- verse.

"Hey, that's strange," said Arx, looking at a computer screen. "We're *still* dragging along that meteor we bumped into."

"Never mind boring old meteors," said Teggs brightly. "Who's for another game of I Spy?"

The days dragged on. But at the end of the

second week, they could at last see Platus Two on the scanners.

And Arx made a strange discovery.

He called everyone to the flight deck to tell them about it.

"Well, Arx?" said Teggs, settling back into the control pit after a long doze.

"I've been studying Platus Two closely, Captain," the triceratops announced. "And something's wrong. I've checked my findings against the notes made by the Jurassic Explorers— and they're completely different!"

Teggs frowned as he chewed some moss. "Different in what way?"

42

Arx looked at him. "Since the Jurassic Explorers visited Platus Two, it has grown *ten times bigger*!"

"Impossible!" Sog said crossly. He tried to cross his arms but they wouldn't quite reach, which made him even crosser. "Planets do not grow like living things! Arx, you must be wrong! Your instruments are faulty!"

At that, Arx got a bit huffy, and Teggs quickly butted in before a big row started.

"Can you show us Platus Two on the scanners, Arx?" he asked.

Arx jabbed a button with his horn. On the screen Platus Two glowed bright against black space. Pure white and smooth, it looked like a giant pool ball.

Then a small rocky shape drifted into view.

"It's that stupid meteor again," grumbled Arx.

"But I thought it was trailing behind us," said Teggs. "How come it's now heading *straight for us?*"

A split second later Teggs got his answer. Everyone jumped as the meteor suddenly split right open! Bursting from inside it—like a terrifying creature hatching from a giant egg—was a familiar whisklike ship.

"Oviraptors!" gasped Gipsy.

Arx nodded grimly. "They disguised their ship as a meteor and tagged along all the way here!"

"They want our eggs!" wailed Coo.

"Oh, dear," said Dippa.

Suddenly the oviraptor ship fired its lasers. Two balls of flame streaked toward them.

"Red alert!" shouted Teggs. "We're under attack!"

Chapter Five

LIGHTNING STRIKES TWICE

Twin bolts of fire slammed into the *Sauropod*. The ship shook like jelly in an earthquake. Then it tipped up. Coo and Dippa screamed, their egg boxes clanging together like giant bells. Professor Sog was sent somersaulting up to the ceiling. The dimorphodon flight crew screeched and flapped into one another.

Teggs fought to keep his balance in the control pit. Flapping reptiles crashed over his head. The squawk of the alarm pterosaur echoed round the ship: *"Red alert! Red alert!"*

"Damage report!" cried Teggs.

Iggy came tumbling out of the elevator and onto the flight deck. "Message from the engine room, Captain!" he yelled. "Engines have been hit!"

"We can't get away now!" cried Sog, as a pair of flying reptiles helped him down from the ceiling.

"Fire lasers," snapped Teggs.

"Lasers have jammed!" Gipsy reported.

"All right then, fire the dung torpedoes!" he ordered.

Gipsy flicked a row of switches with her tail. "Firing now!"

On the scanner a brown explosion lit up the oviraptor ship.

"Direct hit!" cheered Arx.

"That should cause a stink on the oviraptor ship!" Iggy said, and grinned.

"Message coming in," Gipsy reported. "It's King Albu!"

"Put him on-screen," Teggs said.

Everyone watched as an ugly, stubby little creature appeared on the screen. He wore a large crown on his head and an even larger clothes peg on his snout.

Teggs smiled grimly. "I see that you've felt—and smelled—what our dung torpedoes can do, King Albu. Leave now, and we'll say no more about it."

King Albu shook his head. "Doo hab dumfing I vant, Dap-tin," he growled.

"Er . . . pardon?" asked Teggs.

The royal oviraptor pulled the peg from his nose. "I said, you have something I want, Captain!" he gasped.

"You really came all this way just to eat the plateosaurus eggs?" Teggs shook his head sadly. "You have to be crazy!"

"I certainly am," King Albu agreed. "So hand them over—or else my lasers will turn you into toast!"

Teggs shook his head. "Try that, and the next round of dung torpedoes will knock your noses clean off!"

"I don't think so, Captain." King Albu smiled nastily. "Your engines run on dung, and we've just blasted them open. You can't afford to waste any more fuel."

Iggy sighed. "He's right, Captain!"

"Oh, well," sighed Coo. "I suppose we'd better let him have the eggs, then."

"Yes, that's probably best," agreed Dippa. "Never mind."

"Never mind?" Teggs stared at them. "This is the future of your species we're talking about!"

"But there's nothing we can do," said Coo.

"There's always *something* we can do," said Teggs bravely.

"Like what?" asked Professor Sog.

Everyone looked at Teggs.

"Well . . . we need to repair our engines. And for that we need to land." He nodded firmly. "We must head for Platus Two. Now!"

"But we can't outrun King Albu, Captain!" said Iggy.

"We have to try!" Teggs snapped. "We might just lose them by staying in the clouds for a while. Maybe we'll buy enough time to fix the damage."

"It's a brave plan, Captain," said Arx with a small smile.

Gipsy clapped her claws together and called to the flight crew. "Let's do it, team!"

The *Sauropod*'s engines hummed weakly. With a lurch they were off.

"Don't say I didn't warn you, Captain!" snarled King Albu. He put the clothes peg back on his nose and turned to his crew. "Dopen vire!" he shouted.

"Eh?" Teggs frowned.

An earsplitting explosion ripped through the *Sauropod*. The whole ship shook even harder than before.

"He said, 'Open fire,'" said Arx helpfully.

"Approaching Platus Two," said Gipsy. "Entering clouds now."

"Take that raptor off the screen!" said Teggs. "Let's have a look!"

King Albu's evil face was replaced by a close-up view of the white cloudy planet.

"Take us in low," Teggs ordered. "We'll try to steer round behind him and stay out of sight."

"Such a shame," sighed Sog. "We're already

fighting over this calm and peaceful world."

"Er . . . calm and peaceful, you say?" echoed Teggs, looking at the screen.

They'd broken through the clouds. Now they could see what the planet was really like.

It was horrible.

The pale ground was smooth and speckled, but crisscrossed with huge cracks as though it were ready to fall apart. There were no hills or trees, no flowers or animals. Everywhere was flat and featureless, and a fierce storm was raging overhead. Lightning hurled bright daggers down at the ground. Great fountains of sticky lava spurted up to the clouds in revenge.

Dippa sighed. "Not very green, is it?"

"But—but this is terrible!" squawked Professor Sog. "The explorers planted seeds! Why haven't they grown?"

"Now will you believe me?" said Arx. "This can't be Platus Two at all. It's a different world!"

"No!" Sog insisted. "I checked the star charts!

This is right where Platus Two should be!"

Coo and Dippa just stared sadly at the screen.

"Captain!" shouted Gipsy. "The oviraptors have found us! Look!"

King Albu's ship was swooping out of the clouds toward them.

"We have to go faster!" Teggs cried.

"We can't!" yelled Iggy.

Then, just as everything seemed hopeless, a jagged blast of yellow light struck the oviraptor ship. The ship fell from the sky like a stone.

"Lightning!" beamed Teggs. "King Albu's ship has been struck by lightning!"

"Serves them right," said Iggy.

"We're saved!" Professor Sog did a little victory jig. "Yippee!"

But suddenly the scanner glowed white-hot. A crisp crackling noise rasped through the air. Sparks flew around the flight deck. Sog stopped dancing, and the dimorphodon flapped round in panic.

"Oops," said Arx. "Now *we've* been struck by lightning!"

The engines spluttered and died.

"We're going down!" shouted Iggy.

"Attention, crew!" Teggs yelled. "Brace yourselves! We're going to crash!"

"We're going to crash!" squawked the alarm pterosaur. *"We're going to crash!"*

On the scanner the ground came rushing up to meet them. . . .

Chapter Six

THE MYSTERIOUS PLANET

Ka-Boom! Tumbling out of control, the *Sauropod* scraped against the smooth surface of the planet.

B-B-B-B-B-B-B-B-Bang! The ship flipped up and over. It splattered through one of the red-hot geysers spurting out of the ground.

"She can't take much more!" howled Iggy.

"Neither can we!" gasped Dippa.

A long, wide crack had opened up beneath them. The *Sauropod* fell through the crack and started bouncing back and forth against the sides. Then a fresh spurt of sticky lava pushed them high up into the air.

Teggs braced himself. "What goes up must come down!"

At last the final crash came.

No one on board the *Sauropod* had ever heard a noise like it.

It was a crumpling, rumpling, bone-crushing, head-mushing, grinding, grueling, wrenching, bottom-clenching *smash*.

Then the ship was still.

Slowly Coo raised his long aching neck. "I wish I'd stayed at home," he sighed.

"Now we know how the meteor felt when it smashed into Earth," groaned Teggs.

Professor Sog peered out from under a chair. "The eggs!" he twittered. "Dippa, Coo—what about the eggs?"

The two plateosaurus checked their egg boxes.

"Unscrambled," Dippa reported.

"Wish I could say the same for my brains," said Teggs.

Iggy waddled over to the communicator. "Calling

engine room, this is Iggy. Are you all right, boys?"

Assorted moans and groans came from the speaker. "Just about!" someone said.

"Good," said Teggs. "Everyone's okay. But remember, if *we* made it through the landing, chances are that King Albu and his egg-snatchers did too." He hungrily uprooted an enormous fern and swallowed it down. "And there's nothing like a really big crash for working up an appetite!"

"Perhaps we should *all* get eating," said Arx gravely. "We need to make more fuel for the engines."

"Of course," said Gipsy, wrinkling her nose. "More dung!"

"It's a big job," said Teggs. "*Several* big jobs, in fact."

"Leave it to me and my boys," said Iggy, smiling. "We'll have a good meal while we fix the engines. Then we'll fill them up for you—no sweat!"

Teggs saluted him. "I knew I could count on you!"

Iggy saluted in return, and left the flight deck.

Gipsy pulled a face. "Well, while Iggy gets to the *bottom* of things in the engine room, I'll try to listen in on the oviraptors"

"Good idea," said Teggs. "We might learn what they're planning."

Gipsy's hands flicked over the controls. Suddenly a spooky wailing sound crackled out of the speakers.

"What is *that*?" asked Teggs.

"Sounds like a ghost!" said Dippa.

"Or faulty speakers," Arx added.

"I think it sounded like someone in distress," said Gipsy. She pressed some more buttons. "Yes, I've got a fix on the signal now. It's coming from somewhere out on the planet's surface!"

"Impossible!" snapped Professor Sog. "How could anyone live in this terrible place?"

"We'd better find out," said Teggs. "Because if we can't get the ship fixed—we'll be joining them!"

The crew got ready to go outside.

Then they gathered at the ship's main hatch-way.

Teggs had changed into his battle armor, and Gipsy had slipped on her combat suit. If it came to a fight, they would be ready.

Gipsy joined Teggs as he stared out at the strange, dark planet.

"Do you think we'll really get out of this mess?" she whispered.

"We've got to, Gipsy," said Teggs softly. He gave her a crooked smile. "I can't stop exploring space yet! I haven't discovered my very own star dragon!"

"Speaking of discoveries," said Arx, shuffling

over, "I wonder what we'll find out there."

"Well, whoever was making that noise, we can find them with this," said Gipsy, tapping a gadget on her wrist. "It's a special tracker. The faster it bleeps, the closer we are."

"Why can't we just hide on the *Sauropod* until Iggy's fixed the engines?" asked Dippa.

Teggs shook his head. "If the oviraptors come aboard, they'll sniff out the eggs in seconds. Out there in the storm, it will be harder to find the eggs. Besides, Iggy and the boys have some important jobs to do. They mustn't be distracted by a load of rotten reptiles running about."

Just then, a flash of lightning lit up the sky. Gipsy thought she caught a glimpse of something moving just outside.

"We'd better get going," she said nervously.

Teggs led the way out onto the surface of the unpleasant planet, through the howling wind and the drenching rain. The ground was smooth and slippery beneath their feet. He had the feeling they were being watched.

Lightning flashed again. Teggs caught a sudden movement from the corner of his eye—dark shapes, small and nasty, creeping toward them.

"Look out!" he yelled. "It's the oviraptors!"

"It sure is," gurgled Goopo.

"Worst luck for you!" snarled King Albu.

He snapped his claws, and his sons rushed to form a tight circle around the dinosaurs. Teggs saw now that each of them held a ray gun.

"We're trapped!" gasped Gipsy.

Arx lowered his horns. "I could charge them, Captain."

"They'd blast you before you got close," hissed Teggs. "I won't let them add roast triceratops to their mad menu!"

"Now then, Captain Teggs," said King Albu. "You know what I want: eggs!" A dreamy look came into his tiny eyes. "Yes, I said eggs! E-G-G-S. Eggs, eggs, eggs, eggs, eggs." He started drooling. "Eeeeeggsss, mmmmmm."

One by one his sons started dribbling too.

"Eeeeggsss," they echoed.

But not Prince Shelly. He threw down his gun crossly. "This is *silly*, Father!" he complained. "Our ship's lying in pieces! We're stranded billions of miles from home! And all you care about are a few lousy eggs!"

"Lousy?" gasped King Albu in shock. "You dare . . . to call eggs . . . *lousy*?"

The oviraptors all booed and hissed at Prince Shelly.

While they were distracted, Teggs struck.

He lashed out with his armored tail. Blue sparks shot from the end, and four of the little reptiles were sent flying.

"Now, Arx!" Teggs cried.

The triceratops charged at Prince Goopo, who cried out in terror and ran. He screeched so loudly that the others dropped their guns as they scrambled to block their ears.

Then Gipsy sprang into action. With a few well-placed jabs, kicks, and tail-swipes, she flattened five more of the oviraptors.

But King Albu had grabbed one of the ray

guns. He started firing wildly. Bolts of white light sizzled through the air.

"Run!" cried Teggs as one of the laser beams whistled past his ear.

Rushing for cover, Arx and Coo went one way while Gipsy and Sog went another. Dippa ran off all by herself, so Teggs chased after her.

"Just you wait, acorn-brain!" roared King Albu. "I'll get those eggs yet!"

"Not if I can help it," muttered Teggs. He swung his head about wildly, looking for somewhere to hide from the gunfire. But the landscape was smooth and flat on all sides.

"Look out!" called Dippa.

Teggs skidded to a stop just in front of a huge gash in the ground. It was too wide to jump over.

"We'll have to turn back!" wailed Dippa.

"We can't!" said Teggs. As if to prove it, a laser beam whizzed past between them. "There's only one place we can go now!"

Teggs was pointing to the crack in the ground. "Down *there*?" Dippa gulped.

"Now!" cried Teggs.

Together the two dinosaurs leaped into the blackness.

Chapter Seven

THE TUNNELS OF FEAR

Luckily, Teggs and Dippa didn't have far to fall. They landed with a thump on a small ledge.

"Did you know this was here?" gasped Dippa.

"Er . . . of course!" said Teggs quickly.

Dippa peered over the edge. "How deep is this crack?" she wondered. "And what's at the bottom of it?"

A spooky wailing noise rose up from the darkness. It was the same noise they had heard back on the *Sauropod.*

"Who needs Gipsy's tracker?' said Teggs. "Whatever that thing is, it's right beneath us!" He explored along the ledge a little farther. Soon the winking lights on his battle helmet lit up a jagged gash in the smooth rock beside him. "It's another crack . . . a sort of passageway! Come on, before the oviraptors find us."

"I don't like scary passageways," whispered Dippa. "Why don't we just let King Albu *have* the eggs?"

Teggs stared at her. "How can you

even think such a thing?"

Dippa shrugged. "It would be much easier."

"It would be easier, but it would be *wrong*," said Teggs sternly. "Those eggs hold the future of your species! Isn't that worth fighting for?"

"Fighting ruined our old world," said Dippa. "Fighting is bad."

"But giving up is bad too, Dippa," Teggs told her. "I know you're scared. I am too! But you mustn't throw away your dreams."

Dippa nodded slowly. "I dream of a new place to call home," she said. "I dream of having little baby plateosaurus to look after. I dream that one day there will be a whole happy herd of us on our own planet."

"Then *fight* for those dreams," Teggs told her.

Just then, they heard a scuttling sound above them. "This way, boys!" came a familiar wicked voice. "There's a ledge! They must have jumped down here!"

"King Albu!" growled Teggs. "Quick! Let's get going!"

He and Dippa started galloping through the darkness on all fours. The oviraptors soon figured out where they had gone, and gave chase.

"They're catching up!" panted Dippa.

"Keep running!" cried Teggs.

Then the mysterious ghostly wail started up again, chilling them to the bone. Teggs and Dippa skidded to a halt, and so did the oviraptor princes. Teggs saw them by the light of his battle helmet, clutching each other in fear.

"We—we *have* to go back now, Father!" stammered Shelly.

"Never!" cried King Albu. "Now grab those eggs, boys—or I'll hard-boil you all!"

Goopo and his brothers slowly advanced on the two herbivores.

"Get behind me, Dippa," whispered Teggs. "Maybe I can scare them off." He flexed his armored tail, ready to fight. But the passage was too small, and his tail was too big. It whacked against the smooth wall, and suddenly the whole passageway started to shake.

"Look out, Dippa!" shouted Teggs. "The walls are caving in!"

"Eeek!" squeaked Goopo. He turned and fled, his brothers close behind. Teggs and Dippa huddled together as big speckled slabs kept on falling. Soon the passage was completely blocked. They were cut off from the oviraptors—but now there was no way back to the *Sauropod*.

"There's only one path we can take now," said Teggs quietly. "But it'll lead us right to whatever's been making that terrible noise!"

Meanwhile, Gipsy and Sog were huddled outside in a howling gale, wishing they were warm and safe back on the *Sauropod*. Like Teggs and Dippa they had hidden in one of the great splits in the planet's surface. But the ledge they were creeping along was very narrow. One slip, and they would fall to their doom.

"I wonder what caused all these cracks," said

Sog nervously. "If it was an earthquake, where's all the rubble? There's not a single loose stone round here!"

"Maybe it's special supertough rock," said Gipsy. "That's why the explorers' seeds never grew here." Gipsy's tracker started beeping loudly. "You know, this thing is going crazy. It reckons the source of that signal is . . . everywhere!"

"Shhh!" gasped the little professor. "I think something's coming!"

He was right. Something heavy was creeping along the ledge in the opposite direction—straight toward them.

"It's too dark!" hissed Gipsy. "I can't see what it is!"

"It's the thing that made that terrible wailing noise!" cried Sog. "I know it is!" He hopped onto Gipsy's tail and scampered up to her shoulder in fright.

The footsteps shuffled closer and closer. . . .

Chapter Eight

THE SECRET OF PLATUS TWO

"Halt!" squawked Professor Sog bravely. He peered out from behind the crest on Gipsy's head. "Who goes there?"

A familiar figure came out of the shadows. "Hello, Gipsy! Professor!"

"Arx!" squealed Gipsy in delight.

"And me!" called Coo from somewhere behind him.

"Thank goodness!" gasped Sog. "So, you hid in the crack too!"

"There was nowhere else to go," said Arx. He seemed a little out of breath. "I'm glad we've found you. There's something I think you should see."

"What is it?" asked Gipsy.

But Arx was already tracing his footsteps. "The path gets very steep down here. Don't slip!"

Gipsy and Sog followed them along the ledge. Arx was right—the path dipped down sharply. Gipsy trod carefully, while Sog slithered down on his bottom.

The air grew warmer. The ledge grew wider. A soft thudding noise seemed to echo up from the chasm beside them.

To Gipsy it sounded like a huge, heavy heartbeat. Her tracker bleeped so loudly she had to turn it off.

They crept on for what felt like ages. Then the steep path leveled out. Arx came to a sudden stop.

"Here we are," he said. "A hole. I think it stretches down to the very center of the planet!"

Gipsy stared down into the hole. This was the source of the heartbeat sound: *Ba-DUMP . . . Ba-DUMP . . . Ba-DUMP . . .*

It was like looking into a deep well. Far below, thick yellow liquid sloshed about like runny custard.

"Keep watching," Arx murmured.

Then, just below the slimy surface of the yellow goo . . . something massive moved!

"What was that?" Gipsy gasped.

"I think I know," said Arx. "But if I'm right, we're in worse trouble than we thought!"

Even as he spoke, the wall behind them exploded with a mighty crash!

Coo yelped in surprise as bits of the strange smooth rock flew through the air. Sog hid behind Arx's head for safety.

Gipsy whirled around in surprise. "Look!" she cried. A huge hole had appeared in the smooth wall. "Something's coming out!"

A familiar orange head poked out of the darkness. "Only me!"

"Captain Teggs!" Gipsy beamed, and quickly saluted. "And Dippa! You gave us a fright!"

"Sorry about that," said Teggs. "We were walking through one of the cracks, but it came to a dead end."

"So he smashed through the rock with his tail!" added Dippa.

"Rock, eh?" said Arx. He nudged a fragment of the smooth rock with his horn. "I'm not so sure . . . see how easily this stuff breaks?"

Teggs looked hurt. "Well, I did give it quite a whack, you know!"

"I'm sure you did, Captain," said Arx quickly.

"But look at it! So smooth, so brittle. It's not really like rock at all, is it?"

Everyone stared at the broken pieces on the ground.

"You're right," said Teggs slowly. "In fact, it looks a lot like . . . *eggshell*!"

"Eggshell?" twittered Sog. "But this material covers the whole planet!"

"I don't get it," said Coo. "How can a planet be made from eggshell?"

"Easy," said Arx. "Because Platus Two *isn't* a

planet after all! It's an *egg*! A SPECIAL, GIGANTIC, PLANET-SIZE EGG!"

Everyone stared at him in amazement.

"Of course!" breathed Teggs. "It makes perfect sense!"

"Seems crazy to me," said Dippa.

"Ah, but things aren't always as they seem," said Teggs. "Remember the way the oviraptor ship was hidden inside the meteor? This is the same idea—only there's something a lot bigger hidden inside this planet!"

Arx turned to Professor Sog. "I *told* you Platus Two had grown!" he cried. "It's probably been getting bigger and bigger for hundreds of years—because the creature *inside it* has been growing in size too!"

"But—but eggs don't grow!" protested Sog.

"This is no ordinary egg," said Arx. "Besides, can *you* imagine laying an egg the size of a planet?"

"Ouch!" Teggs winced. "That would bring tears to your eyes!"

"So let me get this straight," said Gipsy, excitedly. "The explorers mistook Platus Two for a planet, just like we did. But deep inside it is the biggest baby in the universe—and it's starting to hatch!"

"That's why there are cracks all over the place!" said Teggs. "The thick shell is breaking open!"

"What about those geysers?" asked Coo. "How can an egg spray molten lava everywhere?"

"But it's *not* molten lava," Gipsy told him. "It's just egg white bursting out as the egg starts to hatch!"

"Well, what about that scary noise?" asked Dippa.

"Come on," said Arx, like a stern schoolteacher.

"What's the first thing a baby does when it hatches?"

"It cries!" Dippa realized. "That's what we've been hearing!"

They all stared down into the deep dark hole, where the baby was slowly stirring in its runny yolk.

"Think how big it must be," whispered Sog. "Simply enormous! That movement we saw was probably just an eyelash! Or the tip of a whisker!"

"Uh-oh," said Gipsy. "I just had an awful thought. If this creature really *is* ready to hatch, then Platus Two must be close to completely cracking up!"

"I know how it feels," sighed Coo.

"Guys," said Teggs gravely, "if we can't get off this egg-world—we're doomed!"

"You're right!" Sog squealed. "We'll all be flung off into space!"

"Flung off into space?" said someone behind them. "Ha! That will seem like fun compared to what *I'm* going to do to you all!"

Teggs turned to find King Albu creeping along the ledge toward them, his red eyes agleam. The oviraptors had tracked them down!

"Quick!" Teggs shouted. "Run for it!"

But then Prince Goopo led his brothers out of the shadows, blocking their way.

King Albu giggled with glee. "This time there will be no escape!"

Chapter Nine

A STICKY END

"Listen, you egg-mad maniac," shouted Teggs. "This whole world is about to break apart! We have to get out of here—and fast. If we work together, maybe we can—"

"Nope." King Albu shook his head. "I'm not doing a single thing until I've eaten those eggs. So *nyah*!"

Coo lumbered forward. "All right, then," he said. "I suppose you'd better have them."

"No!" shouted Dippa. "I won't let you!" She slammed her mighty tail down on the ground in front of Coo.

Coo froze. Everyone stared at Dippa in amazement—even King Albu.

"Captain Teggs is right," she said. "Those eggs are our future, Coo. And our future is worth fighting for."

"It is?" Coo blinked in surprise. "Oh. Well, if you really think so . . ."

Dippa smiled at Teggs. "I *know* so."

"You know nothing!" spat King Albu. "Come on! Eggs! Now!"

But even as he spoke, the ground started to shake. A fountain of steaming hot goo burst out from the deep dark hole in the ground.

"See that, King Albu?" Teggs yelled. "That's *egg white.* This whole place is

95

bursting with the stuff! Why are you bothering with a few measly plateosaurus eggs? The biggest, rarest egg in the whole universe is right under your feet!"

"Egg white?" King Albu started to drool. "Goopo, taste it at once."

Goopo edged forward, keeping his gun aimed at Teggs. He dipped a long finger in the goop, then sucked it clean.

At once a dreamy smile spread over his face. "It—it's the best egg I've ever tasted!" he shrieked.

Goopo threw away his gun and dived into the sticky stream. It whooshed him right up to the top of the fountain. He balanced there, guzzling the liquid as though it were lemonade.

"Get out of that!" yelled King Albu. "It's mine!"

He jumped into the fountain, which carried him high up into the air. He and Goopo bobbed about on the thick goo together, eating all they could.

"It's true!" shrieked the king. "It's the eggiest

egg-juice I've ever tasted! Come on boys— jump in!"

Prince Hibbit dived into the fountain, and the others followed him, crying for joy. They were like mad birds flapping about in a giant birdbath.

All except Prince Shelly. He stood and stared at his father and brothers in horror.

"Stop it!" he shouted. "You heard Captain Teggs, this whole place is about to break up! We must get out of here!"

But the oviraptors were far too busy filling their faces to listen. They didn't even notice when the fountain got suddenly smaller. . . .

"Albu! Goopo! Look out!" Teggs yelled.

"Get out of there, you lot, quick!" added Shelly.

But it was too late.

As quickly as it had come, the egg-white fountain dried up to a dribble. As the thick liquid fell away, for a moment King Albu and his boys were left dangling in midair. Then, with a loud yell, they fell—right down into the deep hole.

"It must be miles down to the bottom!" said Arx.

They heard a quiet distant splash. And then the scary wailing noise started up again. "Put me down!" they heard King Albu squawk in the distance. "I'll have you poached in butter for this!"

But then a terrible munching sound filled the air.

"The egg strikes back," said Teggs grimly.

"I tried to stop them," sighed Shelly.

"You did everything you could," Gipsy agreed.

"Come on," said Arx. "That thing is waking up, and it's hungry. We don't want to wind up as pudding!"

"You're right," said Teggs. "There's no time to lose."

"What about him?" Dippa scowled at Shelly. "If he comes with us, he might eat our eggs!"

Shelly shook his head. "Believe me, I've lost my appetite!"

"Enough talk," yelled Teggs. "Back to the *Sauropod*! RUN!"

They ran for their lives.

The egg-planet rumbled and shook. Geysers

of egg white spurted up all around them. The sky was darker than ever, and it was hard to see anything very clearly.

But they managed to find their way back to the ship.

"Iggy!" yelled Teggs, panting for breath in the doorway. "Are you there?"

"Phew!" gasped Sog. "What's that terrible smell?"

"Must be Iggy and the boys," said Gipsy.

"They've been working hard on our dung problem!"

Iggy appeared round the corner. He looked tired and red-faced, and his scaly hide was dripping with engine oil.

"We need to take off straightaway," said Teggs. "Is that okay?"

Everyone stared at Iggy, hope burning in their eyes.

"Sorry, Captain," said Iggy, shaking his head. "We've got all the dung we need, but the engines are still stone cold. And it'll take hours to burn enough dung for takeoff!"

"But we don't have hours!" said Teggs.

Coo hung his head. The precious egg box fell to the floor. "Then . . . we can't escape!" he sighed. "It's all been for nothing!"

Chapter Ten

THE END OF THE EGG

"Wait a minute," said Dippa. "We can't take off, right?"

"Right," said Teggs. She turned to Professor Sog. "And if we stay, we'll be flung off into space like you said, right?"

"It's true," he said sadly. "No one could survive such a thing."

"*We* certainly couldn't,"

Dippa agreed. "But maybe the *Sauropod* could—with us safely inside it!"

Arx hooted for joy. "She's right! There's still a chance! If this jumbo egg is going to hatch, we don't *need* to take off! We'll be flung off into space anyway!"

Teggs grinned at her. "Good thinking, Dippa." He turned to Iggy. "Do you think the *Sauropod* can stand it?"

Iggy shrugged. "She's a tough ship . . . but I just don't know!"

"Well, I think we're about to find out," said Gipsy.

Just outside, a big split in the ground had opened up.

"Quick! Everyone to the flight deck!" yelled Teggs. "Find something to hold on to!"

Minutes later the flight deck was filled to bursting with worried dinosaurs.

Iggy and his ankylosaurs had strapped themselves to the walls. Gipsy, Teggs, and Sog were squashed up in the control pit. Arx stood at his post, studying his instruments. Prince Shelly sat nervously beside him. Dippa and Coo huddled together, clinging to their egg boxes. The alarm pterosaur perched with the flight crew. She gave a nervous squawk now and then.

Everyone had gathered together—perhaps for the last time.

Beneath the ship the ground started to boil and buckle.

"Platus Two is cracking up," Arx reported.

"Hold tight, everybody," Teggs called. "And good luck."

They watched the egg-planet's last moments on the scanner screen.

The cracks in the ground grew wider and darker. They spat sticky goo high into the air. The *Sauropod* rattled and shook.

Then the distant horizon seemed to crack open. Something enormous burst out from beneath. It was groping around as if trying to grab the last stars in the sky.

"It's a claw!" cried Teggs. "A giant claw!"

More and more jagged cracks appeared in the shaking shell.

"This is it!" cried Arx. "Here we go!"

And suddenly there was a terrific *crack!* as the egg-planet burst apart.

The scanner screen glowed white hot. The *Sauropod* was sent spinning. No ship had ever stood up to such incredible force.

"You can do it," Teggs whispered quietly. "I know you can!"

And at last, after what seemed like hours and hours, the shaking and the spinning stopped.

For a long time no one moved. No one even dared to speak.

It was left to Teggs to break the silence. "We made it!" he shouted. "We actually made it!"

The flight deck rang with the sound of happy cheers and squawking.

Cautiously Professor Sog wriggled out from Teggs's armpit. "Look!" he gasped. "On the screen!"

The blackness of space was littered with pieces of broken shell. They gleamed like bits of china in the starlight.

Then something incredible burst into view. It looked like an enormous golden serpent. Its long gleaming body stretched out through the stars like a comet's tail. Slowly it opened its

jaws and breathed out a big ball of fire as bright as the sun.

"Wait a minute," said Arx. "That looks like . . ."

"It can't be!" gasped Sog.

"It is!" cried Teggs. "It's a star dragon. It must be! The Jurassic Explorers searched the galaxy but never found one."

Arx beamed. "And now we've seen one with our own eyes!"

"In honor of my greatest heroes," said Teggs, "I name this star dragon Jurassic."

Jurassic the star dragon performed a slow somersault. Then she flapped away into the endless night on four massive golden wings.

"I'm glad Jurassic hatched safely," said Gipsy

softly. "I wonder where she'll go now."

"To warm herself by a sun, perhaps," suggested Sog. "Or maybe to find her friends in a far-off galaxy. Who knows?"

Iggy smiled. "I'm sure there's a home big enough for her somewhere."

"Maybe we'll see her again someday," said Teggs happily, "and find out for sure."

They watched Jurassic slowly disappear, off on her long journey through the stars. Then

Iggy disappeared too, to check on his precious engines.

"What about us? What about our home?" sighed Coo. "Where can we go with our eggs?"

Dippa smiled. "Cheer up, Coo. Like the star dragon, we'll find somewhere."

Prince Shelly hopped over. "I am so sorry for all the trouble my family caused you. Will you let me try to make it up to you?"

"Good for you, Shelly," said Teggs. "You're a

very unusual ovirap-
tor!"

"That's for sure."
Shelly smiled. "To tell
you the truth . . . eggs cause
me to break out in a rash!"

Arx chuckled. "Hey! You're
now King Albu's only son.
That makes *you* the king!"

"You're right!" Shelly said
thoughtfully. "You know, my family
owns a holiday moon near Pluto Springs.
I went there once, as a hatchling—it's sunny
and grassy and very quiet."

Dippa stared at him. "So?"

"So, I guess it's mine now." He smiled at her
and Coo. "And I'd love to give it to you two!
You can live there for as long as you like."

"Will we be safe from other oviraptors?"
asked Coo.

"I promise," said Shelly. "King Albu's mad

menus are a thing of the past. From now on we'll leave you in peace!"

Dippa grinned at Coo. "Looks like we've got a new home out of this trip after all!"

Suddenly the *Sauropod* lurched forward. The sound of mighty engines firing filled the flight deck.

"Captain!" cried Iggy, jogging up to Teggs. "The heat of that explosion has warmed up the engines. We're ready to go back home!"

"First stop, Pluto Springs!" Teggs said, grinning.

"Oh, I do like a happy ending," cried Arx.

"Me too," said Gipsy as she gave Prince Shelly a hug.

"And the really great thing about one mission ending is that a new mission is never far behind," said Teggs, beaming round at his fine crew. "Whatever it is, I hope it's just as *egg-citing* as this one!"

TALKING DINOSAUR!
How to say the dinosaur names in this book . . .

STEGOSAURUS—
STEG-oh-SORE-us

COMPSOGNATHUS—
komp-sog-NATH-us

PTEROSAUR—
TEH-roh-sore

HADROSAUR—
HAD-roh-sore

OVIRAPTOR—
OH-vih-RAP-tor

TRICERATOPS—

trie-SER-rah-tops

DIMORPHODON—

die-MORF-oh-don

IGUANODON—

ee-GNAH-oh-don

CARNOTAURUS—

KAR-noh-TORE-us

DIMORPHODON—

die-MORF-oh-don

ANKYLOSAURUS—

an-KI-loh-SORE-us

PLATEOSAURUS—

PLAT-ee-oh-SORE-us

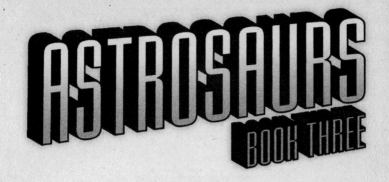

ASTROSAURS

BOOK THREE

The Seas of Doom

READ THE FIRST CHAPTER HERE!

Chapter One

A SOGGY MISSION

"Calling Captain Teggs." Admiral Rosso's gruff voice crackled from the *Sauropod*'s speakers. "Captain Teggs, can you hear me?"

"At last!" beamed Teggs Stegosaur. "Now we'll find out our latest mission."

"And why we've been sent to Aqua 16," said Arx, the gray triceratops beside him. "The soggiest planet in the universe."

Teggs was the captain of the DSS *Sauropod*, the finest ship in the Dinosaur Space Service. He and his crew were all highly trained astrosaurs. They flew through space helping plant-eaters in peril—wherever the planet, whatever the risk.

But why had the *Sauropod* been sent to a world full of *fish*?

Gipsy Saurine trotted over to Teggs. She was a duck-billed hadrosaur whose scaly skin was an eye-catching black and white. "Shall I put the admiral on the scanner screen, Captain?" she asked.

"Please do," said Teggs. He was a young daredevil stegosaurus, eight meters long from tail to beak. Jagged plates of rock-hard armor ran down his orange-brown back.

Gipsy switched on the scanner and Admiral Rosso's wrinkled face appeared. "Ah, there you are, Teggs," said the old barosaurus.

Teggs saluted. "What's up, sir?"

"It's what's *down* that's worrying us," said Admiral Rosso. "Down below!"

Arx and Gipsy swapped puzzled looks. But Teggs just smiled at the thought of a brand-new adventure beginning.

"Something very big and very dangerous is swimming about in the seas of Aqua 16," the admiral went on gravely. "The *Cryptoclidus* who fish there are getting very worried."

Teggs frowned. "Crypto-who?"

"A race of sea reptiles from the planet Cryptos," Arx explained. "They get through tons of fresh fish every day."

"Very good, Arx," smiled Admiral Rosso. "Teggs, you have a first-rate first officer there!"

"He's the best," Teggs agreed. "So, what's been happening on Aqua 16?"

"Five undersea fish factories have been wrecked, along with several submarines." Admiral Rosso sighed. "But no one knows who's doing it—or why."

Teggs nodded. "And you want us to find out."

"That's right," said Admiral Rosso. "The sea reptiles may not be vegetarians, but they are still our friends and neighbors in space.

They've asked us for help in solving this mystery."

"So what are we waiting for?" asked Teggs. He tore a huge clump of ferns from the control pit and swallowed them down in one gulp. "Let's get to Aqua 16 and see what we can find!"

Once Admiral Rosso had given them a map and some orders, Teggs, Gipsy, and Arx went to the shuttle bay. The air was smoky and thick with the smell of burning dung. Iggy Tooth, the *Sauropod*'s chief engineer, was waiting for them by the shuttle.

"The engines are all fired up, Captain," said the stocky iguanodon. "We're ready to go!"

Once they were all safely strapped in, the shuttle blasted off. Then they were soaring through the brilliant blue skies of Aqua 16.

"Wow!" said Teggs, peering through the window. "What a view. There's nothing to see but sea!"

Below them, the green ocean stretched out endlessly to the far horizon. Enormous spaceships floated above the waves, trailing fishing nets behind them. Teggs watched one spaceship rise higher than the rest. Its net was bulging with shimmering, silvery fish that sparkled in the bright sunlight.

"No wonder the *Cryptoclidus* need our help," said Arx. "This is a very big ocean for something nasty to hide in."

"Where are we going to park the shuttle?" asked Iggy.

"On one of their floating factories," said Gipsy, checking her wrist tracker. "It's not far from here."

"It was the first place to be attacked," said Teggs. "We'll take a look and search for clues."

Soon the floating factory came into sight. It looked like a large square of shiny metal, covered in long huts and shacks. In the middle of the square, a small gray shape started waving at them.

"Who's that?" asked Iggy, as they came in to land.

"That must be Commander Cripes," said Arx. "He'll be showing us around."

The shuttle landed safely, and its doors slid open. A strong smell of salty fish filled the air.

As the dinosaurs stepped outside, Cripes came waddling up to greet them. Like all *Cryptoclidus*, he looked like a cross between a seal and the Loch Ness Monster. He had a long neck and four flat flippers, and his belly dragged on the ground as he moved. A broad-brimmed hat was perched on his head, and a shiny cape kept the sun off his long, smooth back.

"Welcome to Aqua 16, guys," said Cripes. "Admiral Rosso told us to expect you. Glad you could make it!"

"Thanks," said Teggs. "This is Arx, and this is Iggy."

Cripes smiled. "And this cute little hadrosaur just *has* to be Gipsy." He took her hoof in his flipper and kissed it. "Now, let me show you around. This factory stretches down almost to the seabed. . . ."

Cripes led them into a large elevator. It took them down at least a dozen levels. When it finally stopped, Teggs led the way out into a large, crumbling workplace. The machines and conveyor belts stood silent. The walls were cracked. The floor was flooded with smelly, oily water.

"We used to pack up the fish for sending home in here," said Cripes. "It was such a lively place. Full of bustle and noise."

Arx plodded over to a wall and prodded a button with his longest horn. Everyone jumped as the machines sparked into life. Pistons turned. The conveyor belt jerked forward. Metal scoops swung down from the wonky ceiling.

"Brilliant!" shouted Teggs over all the noise. "The machines still work!"

"That's right," cried Cripes. "The fish plop out of this pipe here onto the conveyor belt. Then they're wrapped up in the wrapping machine." He sighed. "But the rooms below were ruined in the attack. This whole place will have to be rebuilt."

They watched the noisy machines at work. Then suddenly the ground shook beneath their feet.

"That's not the builders starting work already, is it?" asked Gipsy nervously.

At once, the whole factory rocked as if a giant had kicked it. The astrosaurs were knocked off their feet. The cracks in the walls widened. The floor broke open beneath them, and seawater began rushing in.

"Never mind the builders!" cried Teggs over the din of the machines and the churning water. "I think whatever attacked this place before has come back to finish it off!"